Jake's Toad House

written by Barbara Kanninen

illustrated by Lisa Fields

KAEDEN BOOKS™

"Hi, Jake," said Kim. "What are you doing with that flower pot?"

"It's not a flower pot," said Jake. "It's a toad house. I made it."

Kim looked around. "Where is the toad?" she asked.

Jake rested his chin in his hands. "I'm waiting for one to come."

"Hmm," said Kim. "Maybe it would come if you had food. Do you want me to get some?"

"Sure," said Jake. "Thanks."

Kim brought a dish of apples. She set it near the house and sat down next to Jake. She rested her chin in her hands.

"Now a toad will come," said Kim.

The two children waited.

"Hi, Jake. Hi, Kim," said Robert. "What are you doing?"

"We're waiting for a toad," said Kim. "Jake made a house. I brought apples."

Robert shook his head. "Toads don't eat apples. They eat bugs."

"Gross," said Kim.

Robert looked around. "What about water? Everyone needs water. Do you want me to get some?"

"Okay," said Jake. "Thanks."

Robert brought a cup of water and set it near the house. He sat down next to Jake and Kim and rested his chin on his hands.

"Now a toad will come," said Robert.

The three children waited.

"Hi, Jake. Hi, Kim. Hi, Robert," said Maria. "What are you doing?"

"We're waiting for a toad," said Robert. "Jake made a house. Kim brought food. I brought water for the toad to drink."

Maria shook her head. "I read about toads in a book. They don't drink water. They sit in it. The water goes through their skin."

"Cool," said Robert.

Maria looked around. "Why don't you put the house next to that old log? Toads like dark places. I read that too."

"Good idea," said Jake. He moved the house into the shade.

11

Kim and Robert ate the apples.

Maria poured the water from the cup to the dish and sat down next to Jake, Kim, and Robert.

"Now a toad will come," said Maria.

The four children rested their chins in their hands.

They waited and waited.

"Children, time to go home for dinner!" called Jake's mom.

"Oh, well," said Maria.

"Too bad a toad didn't come," said Robert.

"Yes, too bad," said Kim.

"Bye," said Jake. "Thanks."

The children went home.

15

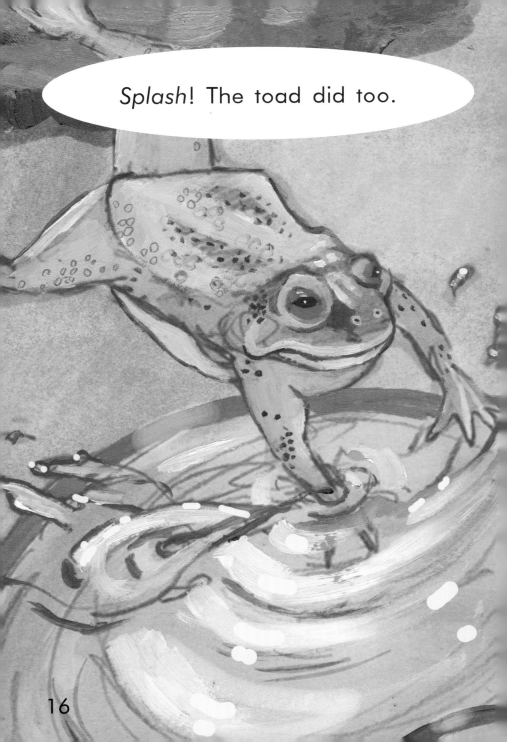